D0426294

The Night Before Dog-mas

By
Claudine Gandolfi

Illustrated by
Karen Anagnost

PETER PAUPER PRESS, INC.
WHITE PLAINS, NEW YORK

Designed by Arlene Greco
Illustrations copyright © 1998
Karen Anagnost

Text copyright © 1998
Peter Pauper Press, Inc.
202 Mamaroneck Avenue
White Plains, NY 10601
ISBN 0-88088-835-0
Printed in China
14 13 12 11 10 9

Visit us at www.peterpauper.com

The Night Before Dog-mas

'Twas the night before Dog-mas,

when all through the pound

not a puppy was yelping,

or playing around;

Our leashes were hung

by our kennels with care,

in hopes that St. Bernard

would soon find us there;

Chihuahuas were curled up,

all snug in their beds,

while visions of doggie-treats

danced in their heads;

Max in his collar,

on somebody's lap,

had tucked in his tail

for a midwinter's nap,

When outside the room

there arose such a clatter,

my ears perked right up

to hear what was the matter.

Away to the window

I jumped up with glee,

and barked at the shadows

that were cast by a tree.

The glow from the moon

changed night into day,

and started me thinking,

"Woof, woof! Time to play!"

When, what with my puppy-dog

eyes did I see,

But a splendid dog-sled,

led by doggies like me,

With a regal furred driver

commanding, not stern.

I yelped to the others,

"That must be St. Bern!"

More rapid than greyhounds

our saviors they came,

and we barked and we howled,

and called them by name:

"There's Duchess!

There's King!

fat Chance,

and bare Buffy!

On Fido! On Scooter!

On, Rover and Scruffy!

Go by the red hydrant

and run past those trees!

Nothing can stop you,

not even some fleas!"

As puppies at play

chase after a stick

and race to their masters

so lively and quick,

So out in the field

his canines all flew,

catching the Frisbees,

that St. Bernard threw.

And then in an instant,

I heard at the door

the scratching and clawing

of each little paw.

As I pulled in my nose,

and was turning around,

Through the door St. Bernard

came in with a bound.

He was dressed all in fur,

from his head to his tail,

his wood cask adorned

with an icing of hail;

A bag of chew-toys he had

brought in with him,

and his mouth was turned up in

what looked like a grin.

His eyes-how they twinkled!

his ears flopped, how merry!

His coat shone like crystal,

his nose like a cherry!

His big sloppy mouth

was drawn up like a bow,

and the fur on his chin

was as white as the snow;

The stump of a bone

he held tight in his teeth,

and his collar encircled

his neck like a wreath;

He had a large face

and a furry, round belly

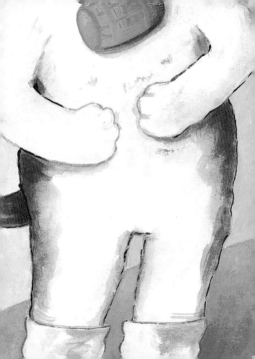

that shook when he barked,

like a bowl full of jelly.

He was fluffy and plump,

a big, cuddly old pooch

and I laughed when I saw him

and gave him a smooch.

A wink of his eye and

a wag of his tail;

we knew right away

we'd have homes,

without fail.

He howled not a howl, but

went straight to his deed,

and took down our leashes

that soon we would need.

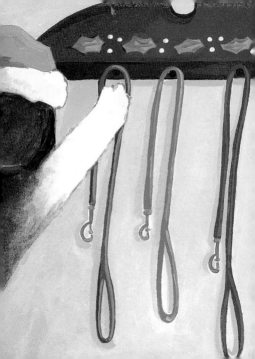

He opened the door,

and families stood there,

with children, all smiling,

and much love to spare.

He leapt to his sled,

to his team gave a call,

and away they all flew

as if chasing a ball.

But I heard him exclaim

as he chewed on a bone:

"Happy Dog-mas to all
and to all a Good Home!"